D1544493

SPACE CAT
VISITS VENUS

SPACE CAT

VISITS VENUS

by RUTHVEN TODD

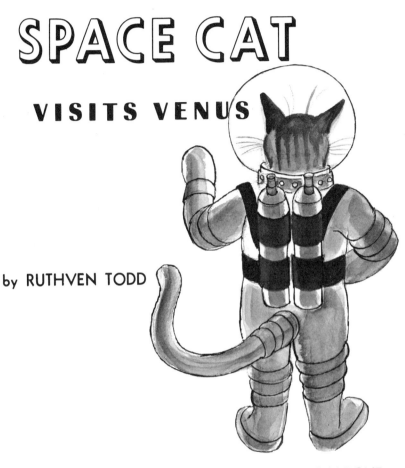

Illustrated by PAUL GALDONE

CHARLES SCRIBNER'S SONS   NEW YORK

SPACE CAT

VISITS VENUS

CHAPTER
ONE

Flyball was the only cat in Luna Port, the first city built on the Moon. He was the only cat on the whole Moon. And he was a famous cat, for with his friend Captain Fred Stone, now Colonel Stone, he had travelled on the first rocket ever to go from Earth to the Moon.

In those days Flyball had been little more than an adventuresome kitten. Now he had become a large and handsome grey cat. He knew his way around Luna Port, under the great bubble of plastic, just as well as any of the men, and each day he went on several tours of inspection. Nobody dared to take things easy when he was around, and he was always around, popping up in the most unexpected places. He went about his business with his sleek grey tail stuck up in the air.

Away at one end of the dome many men were at work, putting together a huge new rocket-ship. This one was many times bigger than the one Flyball and Fred Stone had used to reach the Moon the first time. All the pieces of this enormous ship were being carried up from the Earth by other rockets, and were being put together on the Moon because it was much easier to work there, where heavy things became quite light.

Flyball, of course, was most interested in this big ship. He knew that it was being built for him (and, naturally, for Fred Stone) to make a new voyage. This new journey was to be much longer than the mere hop from the Earth to the Moon. They were going to try to reach the planet Venus.

"Going to Venus, pal," Colonel Stone had told Flyball, "will be quite some trip, but it will be interesting if we make it. Nobody knows what we'll find behind those clouds which hide the planet from us!"

Flyball knew that everybody expected him to go along on the trip. They had tried to prevent his journey to the Moon, but he had been too smart for them and had managed to have his own way. This time there would be no nonsense. When the rocket-ship left for Venus, Flyball would be right there, recognized as a full member of the crew.

Day by day the ship grew bigger and bigger. It was being built on a track that led to the wall of the dome, in which there was set a great metal door. Flyball, who knew everything, knew that once the ship was finished the part of the dome where it was being built would be sealed off and the air let out. Then the enormous ship would be pushed and hauled to the landing-ground and set up on its tail, ready for the take-off.

More and more equipment was brought in by each rocket that arrived from Earth. At first, Flyball had inspected each crate as it was unpacked, hoping to find a stowaway mouse. But as he found no mice, he soon knew that if he was to try to examine each one properly, and there were so many of them, he would have to give up his regular tours of duty around Luna Port. He had to be content with spot-checking, and with seeing that the men fitted all the strange-shaped gadgets neatly and properly.

Apart from the ship, there was plenty to occupy Flyball's time. For instance, there was the observatory where, free from the troublesome clouds and soupy atmosphere of Earth, the men had put up a giant telescope. With the help of this they took hundreds and hundreds of photographs and they were forever getting terribly excited.

"Here," one of them would cry, waving a dripping negative in front of a light, "what *do* you think of this?"

Á shaking finger would point out to Flyball
something that looked like a drop of ink in the
millions of other drops of ink against a milky back-
ground that made up a photograph of the sky.
Flyball, who really did not know or care much
about star-gazing, would always twitch his whiskers gravely and approvingly.

He did not want to hurt anyone's feelings by appearing uninterested. If it was a new star or a new planet and they wanted him to go there to inspect it, he was perfectly willing to go.

Just give him the ship (and, of course, Colonel Stone) and he would be off. But Venus came first. It was not so far away and, besides, Flyball had heard so many people talking about it that he felt curious. The distant stars would just have to wait.

Much more interesting than the observatory, though, so far as Flyball was concerned, were the kitchens and the Moon gardens. In the gardens there were miles and miles of troughs filled with water and chemicals in which all sorts of vegetables grew without any soil. Tangled white roots filled the troughs and above were tomatoes, squash, spinach, corn and half a hundred other vegetables. The lights in these gardens were specially arranged to help the vegetables ripen in the shortest possible time.

Flyball noted with faint disapproval that, in the kitchens, there was none of the potato-peeling that had taken up so much time at the experimental station back on Earth. The potatoes here came ready peeled in big cans and all the cooks needed was a can-opener. The men seemed to be glad there was no peeling to be done but, just the same, Flyball felt that a station was not really a station without it. The piling up of empty cans was not at all the same thing as the slow growth of a mound of potato-peelings.

Still, Flyball had to admit that some pretty tasty things *did* come out of cans, even if men had not yet got around to canning fish-heads for the benefit of cats. Sometimes he thought longingly of a good old-fashioned cod's head. In the canned fish there were no bones with which he could wrestle, and a good fish-bone is sometimes a very pleasant thing.

However, when he thought of this, Flyball also remembered that he was a pioneer, and pioneers cannot really expect all the comforts of home. In addition there was the sad fact that there were absolutely *no* mice on the Moon, and in Flyball's opinion, a world without mice was a poor world indeed. He had great hopes for Venus. Maybe there he'd find plenty of mice to chase.

As the time for the flight drew nearer, Flyball would sit watching the men, through the transparent walls of the dome. They were busy raising the giant rocket so that it stood up, pointing toward the sky. On Earth it would have been a hard job to raise this enormous piece of metal, but on the Moon, where nothing weighed much, a job which would have taken masses of tackle and innumerable men could be done with very little by a few men.

Watching the men working on the rocket, Flyball thought the ship looked large enough to carry a crew of at least a dozen. However, he had heard the experts talking and knew that the scientists and engineers had worked out that it could only carry a little more weight than itself and he, along with Colonel Stone, made up that weight.

In fact, they came every week and asked Flyball whether he would oblige them by sitting on a set of scales, just so that they could keep a check on how heavy he was. The Colonel had to do the same. Luckily, the strict rationing and the exercise they took on the Moon meant that they did not vary much in weight. Of course, the men who weighed them had to do arithmetic, for weights on the Moon were very different from those on Earth. On Earth, for instance, the Colonel weighed a hundred and sixty pounds while on the

Moon he barely tipped the scales at twenty-five pounds.

In addition to their weights, Flyball knew that there was also the matter of the fuel which would drive the rocket-ship free of the attraction of the Moon and send it on its way to Venus. On Earth the ship would have needed so much fuel that there would not have been room for Flyball and Fred Stone. It would, Flyball knew, take nearly as much fuel to escape from Venus as it would have done from the Earth, but the fact that it took so little to get away from the Moon meant that they would have plenty of room for extra fuel in case of accidents. Only by going to and from the Moon were they able to carry enough fuel.

This, the first expedition to Venus, was just to be a trial-flight. That was another reason for there being only one man and one cat as crew. There was no point in risking a great many men, or a great many cats, when no one knew what it was going to be like on Venus. The Colonel had volunteered for the journey and, as he had been the first man on the Moon, everyone agreed that he should go. And where Fred Stone went, Flyball went as well.

11

Day by day the rocket grew nearer to completion. Inside it was fitted with all the automatic equipment which would carry the great ship on its way without help from either Flyball or Fred Stone. The reason for this was that no one knew how either of them would stand up to the strain of travelling through space for many days. Everything had to be made simple in case the journey took too much out of the crew.

Some of the time was spent by Fred Stone and Flyball wearing their space-suits and being swung around in a great drum, in preparation for their great adventure. Flyball did not much like this, but knew he had to put up with it. It was impossible to think of Fred Stone departing for Venus without him. A space-flight without Space Cat would be sure to fail!

CHAPTER
TWO

Then came the take-off. After the speeding-up period was over, and they had escaped from even the slight attraction of the Moon, Colonel Fred Stone helped Flyball out of the hammock which had been specially built for him. This hammock was indeed much more comfortable than the makeshift one he had used to his first journey, the trip to the Moon. That one had been made out of all kinds of odds and ends which had been lying around the station, back on Earth. Fred Stone had been sure in those days that the taxpayers would not have been at all pleased to learn that they had had to pay for a hammock for a cat, even for such a distinguished cat as Flyball.

This time, however, it was a different matter, and the Colonel had been allowed to order whatever he wanted for his companion. One of the first things the Colonel had wanted was the best possible hammock for Flyball. He had designed it himself, with the help of expert engineers. It had been custom-built on Earth, with a bed of foam-rubber, concealed springs and even an arrangement of straps which Flyball could, if necessary, fasten and undo for himself.

Even Flyball who, like all cats, considered himself a real expert on comfort, had to admit that it served to perfection. He had hardly felt any discomfort at all while the ship had been getting faster and faster.

Now the power of the rockets had been cut off, for the greater part of the journey would be made under the momentum which they had gathered in escaping from the attraction of the Moon. They were in free-fall, which meant that there was no longer any rightsideup or upsidedown. Fred Stone fixed tiny metal soles to the pads of Flyball's paws. These little metal sandals were really tiny magnets and they allowed Flyball to walk around on the walls, floor and ceiling of the ship, just as if he was strolling on the ground.

The old ship, which had taken them to the Moon, had only a number—the ZQX-1, showing that it was the first model of its especial type of rocket-ship. This great big shining new ship, however, had a name of its own. Before the bow of the ship had been sent up to the Moon, there had been a great ceremony in which the President's wife had broken a bottle of real champagne over it and had christened it the *Halley*. This was in honor of the famous astronomer who had described the comet which is called after him. Everyone hoped that the new ship would be as well-behaved as a comet as it streaked through space.

Now they were on their way to Venus and the *Halley* seemed to be doing everything that had been expected of her. As nearly all the controls were automatic, the Colonel, strapped loosely in his seat, could relax and read. Flyball, anchored by his magnetic sandals to pieces of metal on the Colonel's clothes, lay quietly and purred as he thought of the great adventure and possible mice on Venus.

In addition to the gadgets, such as the gyroscopic tops which held the *Halley* steady on her course, and the electric controls which would open and close shutters over the heavy glass port-holes, there were other things which had been worked out to help them, and, in particular, to help them eat. Colonel Stone had told the story on Earth of how Flyball, going to the Moon, had had to chase blobs of milk which were floating around the cabin, and the designers had done their best to make certain that that would not happen again. Milk was now stored in the ship's refrigerator in little plastic bags and all Flyball had to do was put a tube in his mouth and press gently on the side of a bag with his paw. In this way he was able to drink his milk without spilling it.

As a seasoned space-traveller, for he had been to and from the Moon several times after the first journey, Flyball had become used to the fact that flights through space were really neither exciting nor interesting. It was only during the take-off and the landing that one had to rely on the skill of the pilot, and there was nothing to bother about with Fred Stone at the controls. After the first shock of discovering that one had no weight in space, travel in a rocket-ship was just plain dull.

Flyball was content to drowse and dream of birds, dogs and mice, with an occasional memory of a really good fish-head.

16

There were neither nights nor days aboard the *Halley* once they had got out into deep space. They just had to eat when they were hungry and sleep when they were tired. Every now and then the Colonel would press one of the buttons which worked the electric mechanism which slid the covers back from the ports.

"That's Earth, Flyball," he would say, pointing to a thing rather like a big softball with strange markings on it, or, turning to a bright silver dollar that seemed nearer to them. "That's the Moon!"

Gradually, however, these objects grew smaller and smaller until, in the end, they were no more interesting than the other objects which were scattered around in the sky. Ahead of them, though, the thing which had only been a spot the size of a thumbtack kept growing bigger and bigger. This was Venus and that was where they were going.

Fred Stone became more and more interested in this thing. He examined it every so often through the powerful telescope that was a part of the equipment of the *Halley*. Still he could find no break in the clouds which surrounded it as if it had been an egg loosely wrapped in cotton-wadding.

"Well, Flyball," he said, after one of these in-

18

spections, "I wonder what we'll find behind all that? I can only hope it'll be clear enough for us to make a landing, and that we'll be able to leave the ship without our suits rotting away on our backs! Still," he paused thoughtfully, "there's not much point in guessing when we'll know the answer so soon."

It seemed as though the journey went on for weeks or even for months, for Flyball did not bother with the *Halley's* chronometer, a most fancy-looking clock that not only kept count of hours, but also of days, weeks, months and even years. He just let time flow round him like a river until Fred Stone, who *had* been keeping count of their progress turned to him.

"We should be getting ready," he said, and turned to the closet in which he had shut their space-suits, to prevent them from floating hither and thither round the cabin of the ship. All along they had been careful about dropping things for, otherwise, with no gravity at all, the cabin of the *Halley* would only too quickly have come to look like a floating garbage-dump.

Once they were dressed in the clumsy but necessary suits, they got back into their hammocks.

19

When the Colonel pressed the button that slid back the cover over the forward port, the woolly globe of Venus seemed to fill nearly the whole glass.

Instead of going straight toward the globe, however, as rocket-ships did when getting near the Moon, the Colonel, pressing the firing-studs of the rockets for short bursts of power, aimed the *Halley* toward Venus in a slanting angle.

"We haven't got the faintest idea of what there may be on the other side of all those clouds," he explained. "There may be plains but there may just as well be mountains. If there should be mountains we don't want to try to find out how strong the *Halley* is by bashing her against them. We'll just have to take things easy until we know which way the land lies."

Slowly, circling round the planet, they drew nearer and nearer to Venus. Looking out through the porthole Flyball watched the great woolly clouds and felt they were never going to get among them. Colonel Stone was being most terribly careful. At last, however, he pulled on a lever which started the rockets pulsing evenly.

"Here we go!" he exclaimed. "Now for the plunge!"

Then they were in the clouds.

Fred Stone worked over the control-board for a few moments. He was setting an automatic pilot which, working with the *Halley's* radar, would swing them away from anything solid which might suddenly stick up in their way. Carefully, he studied a number of dials beside him and made neat notes in his logbook.

"It's just as they thought," he remarked. "There's plenty of ammonia here."

One of the dials beside the Colonel was designed to show how far away they were from the surface of Venus. It was a very special kind of instrument and it was most necessary for their safety, as they could still see nothing through the port except swirling purplish clouds. The clouds were charged with ammonia and the dial that showed this had a needle which flickered on the mark of one hundred.

The Colonel did not look too cheerful, for he knew that men could not live in an atmosphere of ammonia. It looked as though their long journey in search of a place where men could live was not going to have any real result.

The *Halley* was getting closer to the surface all the time.

Then, quite suddenly, they were clear of the clouds, in light that, while not bright with sunshine, still managed to be bright with a strange, pale violet color. The feeling that both of them had was rather the same as that they had known when flying airplanes on Earth. There one might be high above the clouds, in bright sunshine, and then go down through the clouds to find that, for quite some distance from the surface, it was clear.

The Colonel was watching the dials with an astonished expression on his face. The flickering needle which had showed the amount of ammonia in the atmosphere was slowly dropping back toward zero. He tapped at it as a man taps at a barometer, but the needle continued its journey back toward its starting place.

He shook his head solemnly and joined Flyball in gazing out of the port. Miles and miles below them lay the surface of Venus. So far as they could see, and they could see nearly the whole of their side of Venus, there were no high mountains, but there certainly were a great number of seas, or great lakes, while all the surface was a mixture of different shades of green.

Fred Stone whistled softly to himself. "That's

odd," he said. "I wouldn't have expected green plants under this light. We'll just have to suppose that the clouds allow all the necessary light-rays to filter through."

The waters of the seas or lakes were an extraordinary deep blue in color. As they came lower, with the Colonel punching buttons as if they were the stops on an organ, firing alternate jets ahead of them, to slow them down, they saw, through the bursts of flame, that what would have been gold or silver sand on the shores of Earth was here a vivid blue, streaked in places with a bright rich red.

All this time Fred Stone had been keeping an eye on the dial which showed them how high up they were from the surface of the planet.

"Well, Flyball," he said at last, "for better or worse, the time has come to try to make a landing. Steady yourself for the bump, boy!"

It seemed as though it took hours for the great rocket-ship to turn its tail toward Venus, and then it seemed to stand still in the air as the rockets pulsed noisily.

For now that they were in an atmosphere the noise was really tremendous, as the rockets had been almost silent in the vacuum around the Moon. They seemed to hang motionless for a long time, but really they were falling, getting slower all the time as the rockets acted as brakes, toward the edge of one of the seas.

Then, with a thud that jarred them in spite of all that foam-rubber and high-tension springs could do, the *Halley* settled on the surface of Venus. She shuddered once or twice as if about to fall over, and both of them held their breaths as if they were afraid that a single puff or sigh might blow her off balance. Then she was steady. They had made a perfect landing and the ship stood ready to take off again once they had collected the information which was the purpose of their journey.

"Made it, Flyball!" The Colonel let go a great sigh of relief. "At least we'll be able to get away if we don't like what we find here!"

CHAPTER THREE

Colonel Fred Stone, clumsy in his space-suit, went carefully round the *Halley*, checking everything, and making certain that nothing had been damaged in the thud of their landing. In the crook of his left arm he carried Flyball, who had never really learned to like a space-suit, curled as comfortably as possible.

The Colonel stopped for a long time before the dials which were supposed to show exactly what kind of atmosphere there was outside the ship and how it was different from that of Earth. Every single dial had its needle pointing at "zero," showing, or so it might be supposed, that the air outside was fit for man and cat to breathe.

It was little wonder that the Colonel looked puzzled and would have scratched his head, if he could have done so through the goldfish-bowl of his helmet.

"All I can think, Flyball," he said at last, "is that all the dials have gone on the blink together. Too much ammonia, or something like that. Still," he paused, looking at them more closely, "they shouldn't have done that. They all have separate leads and aren't tied together in any way. All the same, whatever the answer may be, we won't take any chances. We'll go out in our space-suits and I'll take the chemicals with me and test the atmosphere that way."

From a locker he took a large square box with a handle. The two of them then went through a door and stood in the air-lock. When the Colonel had closed the door behind them, he swung a lever and opened a door in front of them.

The *Halley* had sunk in the blue ground almost up to the door. The sand, which really was little round clear blue pebbles rather than sand, was now only a couple of feet from the bottom of the door.

Flyball, eager as ever, wriggled out of the Colo-

27

nel's arm. It certainly was not a long drop, but he hit the ground with a thud which knocked the wind out of him. He lay there for a moment.

"Miaow," he managed at last, most indignantly but rather feebly. Being a spacecat was a fine occupation but it certainly did have its troubles. One moment one was as light as a feather and the next one felt as though made of solid lead.

"Miaow!" he said again, but more strongly this time.

Colonel Stone was laughing, most unkindly. "Poor old Flyball," he said at last, as he stooped to pick up his winded friend. "Of course you couldn't be expected to know that the gravity of Venus is very nearly the same as that of the Earth. You've gotten so used to the Moon that you've even forgotten what it was like back on Earth! I weigh around a hundred and sixty pounds on Earth and only twenty-five on the Moon. Here I weigh around a hundred and thirty-six pounds. Supposing that you weigh eight pounds on Earth, you are about one and a quarter pounds on the Moon, and nearly seven pounds here. Try to get that into your noggin. You're nearly the same as Earth weight here!"

This information did little to comfort Flyball, who was thinking that *all* planets and moons should have the same gravity.

Fred Stone put him down on his feet again, and he found that walking was not as bad as he had feared it might be after his tumble. He was pleased to note, in fact, that he was still a lighter cat than he had been on Earth, even if he was not quite so much of a thistledown-weight as he had been on the Moon. The blue pebbles upon which he was now walking with such careful dignity were clear and round and shiny, about the size of peas.

Colonel Stone picked up a small handful of the pebbles in his gloved hand and let them trickle idly through his fingers while he looked up the beach toward the deep green beyond it.

Nearest to the edge of the shore there were some trees. They looked rather like the palm-trees of Earth, but their leaves were far more filmy and feathery. In fact they were as delicately lacy as the fronds of asparagus. Then, too, the trunks of these trees were not rough like the trunks of palm-trees at home. They were smooth and appeared polished, shining as if they had been carefully made from ebony and ivory, arranged in diamond-shaped patterns. Beneath these trees a thick jungle made a riot of different shades of green, splashed with brilliant colors, but they were too far away to see what the different plants looked like.

Colonel Stone opened the box he had been carrying and, crouching down over it, started to do experiments with chemicals, while Flyball watched him gravely. He lit a little alcohol lamp and his expression as he did so was surprised. The flame burned with a clear blue and yellow flame, exactly as it would have done back on Earth. Fred Stone shook his head and started mixing different chemicals which he measured out of bottles into test-tubes. He whistled softly to himself as he worked and the sound echoing out of his space-helmet was very odd indeed.

He repeated each experiment several times, but at last, it seemed, he was contented with the results he had found. He put all the test-tubes and bottles back in their places in the box, which had been made of magnesium for the sake of lightness. Then he straightened up.

He paused for a long moment and then, with a quick and sudden movement, started to loosen the wing-nuts which held his helmet in place. He hesitated for another second and then lifted the helmet from his head and took a deep breath of the pure air of Venus.

He turned his head this way and that, breathing evenly, as if waiting to be knocked over by some unknown poison in the air. Nothing happened, so he stooped down and removed Flyball's helmet.

Flyball was delighted. He had never, in spite of all his flights through space, learned to like either his space-suit or his helmet. Globes, such as the helmets were, might be all right for silly creatures such as goldfish, but they really were rather out of place on a sensible cat.

The next thing the Colonel did was to unzip both their suits and take them back into the *Halley*, through the air-lock. There he hung them neatly in their closet.

"It would never do, Flyball," he said seriously as he closed the door of the closet, "for us to come back and find that something had damaged our suits. I suppose we might make out all right without them, but I don't want to try it!"

Walking up the beach, feeling just a little bit lighter than they would have done on Earth, they nearly stumbled over one of the surprising red streaks which they had noticed before they landed on Venus. It turned out to be the edge of a piece of clear deep red crystal, with smooth surfaces which shone as if they had been polished with diamond-dust on a jeweler's wheel.

Fred Stone tried to scratch the surface of the red crystal with the point of the big knife he carried strapped to his belt. The knife made no mark at all.

"Hard, eh, Flyball?" he asked, as he took an object rather like a fountain-pen out of a box from his hip-pocket. He unscrewed the cover and showed Flyball a tiny point. "Well, we'll see what a diamond will do to it!"

The diamond had no more effect than the knife had had. In the end the fine point of the testing-tool snapped off. The Colonel smiled.

"That's it, Flyball, we've found something that's harder than a diamond, and that's the hardest thing on Earth!" he exclaimed. "But how we're to cut off a sample to take back home with us beats me!"

Flyball had no ideas on the subject and, as a matter of fact, was much more interested by the pale, glowing, violet sky, without a sun, which,

so many miles up, tented the whole of the planet Venus from the rest of the Universe. He felt slightly uneasy under such a strange-colored sky.

If anything lived on Venus it was obvious that that thing would naturally think that its home was the only planet, and the only world, for it could never have seen the others shining in the night sky. Flyball wondered whether, under the green leaves, he would be able to find birds against whom to pit his wits.

Just think of it! Venusian birds who had never heard of the cleverness of cat, let alone that of a much superior spacecat!

The truth of the matter, however, was that, although he had chased them on Earth often enough, Flyball had never actually managed to catch a bird. From his point of view, birds were impertinent creatures which challenged him to do his best in a long jump and then gave out sneering twitters as they flew just a little farther than his best jump.

Padding up the beach behind Fred Stone, Flyball, his grey tail stuck up in the air, congratulated himself that he was a cat and so was not expected to carry all sorts of things. The Colonel was hung around like a Christmas tree with equipment. He had a camera, of course, but he was also slung with little boxes into which he expected to put samples of anything he could find. One purpose of their expedition was to bring home strange objects. The scientists back on Earth were waiting eagerly for their return. Everything they carried back with them would be tested and men would try to see where it fitted in relationship to the things of their own world.

As they had expected, looking up from the beach, the jungle under the odd trees was made up of unfamiliar plants. There were vines with smooth purple stems, twisted and turned around one another, which reached up to offer enormous yellow flowers, the size of soup-plates. In the center of each of these flowers was a glowing scarlet ball, spotted with dark brown. Then there were great tall stems of gold with the most extraordinary eight-sided pods which spiralled round the stems rather like the pods of milkweed on Earth, except that the pods, instead of being silvery-grey, were a most beautiful orange in color, with black ribs down the angles.

Rather shorter than these were the emerald-green pompons of a plant with leaves rather like those of iris, silver and cream flowers a bit like columbines, pineapple-like objects with deep purple thorns tipped with bunches of pale violet spurs, and curly green grass which had brighter green flowers.

The oddest thing about the plants, however, was not their appearance but their behavior. As Fred Stone and Flyball drew near them they swayed out of the way as if to avoid being trampled upon. They seemed to be able to pull their roots aside through the ground. And the ground itself was strange; it had a tough rubbery surface, but the plants seemed to find no difficulty in pulling through it, leaving no cracks behind.

It was almost as though the plants were opening a path before them; as if the plants were determined to lead them in one particular direction.

Flyball's whiskers winked briskly, his nose crinkled and every hair on his neck stood up as if he had a bristly collar. There was something most odd about this world and he was not quite sure that he liked it. There was none of the humming of bees, the chirping of crickets or the chomp-chomping of little tree-frogs which he had known on Earth. There was nothing. It was a world of dull plants.

Colonel Stone, also, felt the strangeness of this silent world, but he had a job to do and had unslung his camera. He was intent on taking photographs of all this newness. He did not seem to notice, as Flyball did, that the plants were guiding them. Flyball, knowing that they were going no place in particular, did not think there was any reason why he should draw the Colonel's attention to the swaying and drawing-aside of the strange plants.

In spite of the fact that he was a trifle lighter than he would have been on Earth, Flyball did not cavort or gambol as he usually would have done. In the silence which surrounded him, he had a strange feeling that something was watching him, and, even odder, that people were talking about him. He sniffed but he could smell nothing except the unfamiliar perfumes of the plants. He tried to nibble a piece of grass, as he had done at home, but somehow the grass would not stay there to be nibbled.

Flyball scratched beneath his chin.

Very well, if the grass did not want to be nibbled, he would leave it alone. After all, he was no vegetable-eater.

He tried to rub his side against one of the thin golden stems but that, too, bent out of the way just as he thought he had touched it. An odd world, this, he thought to himself, but then what could one expect of a place that had no real sunshine!

He was trying to persuade himself that everything was as it should be, in spite of the lack of things he knew. When he listened with his sharp ears, and Flyball had very good hearing, he could make nothing out. But, when he stopped listening,

there was a curious buzzing noise *inside his head.* That buzzing had not been there down on the beach, so Flyball knew that it had nothing to do with his having been shut up in the *Halley* or in a space-helmet.

He decided that he would see what happened if he left the path which the obliging plants were opening up before them. He looked hopefully at an opening and made toward it. Before he got there, however, the opening was filled with the pineapple-like plants. Flyball looked at the violet spurs and realized that they were at least as sharp as his own claws. He turned his back on them and pretended he had not thought of leaving the path. Then he turned round suddenly. The opening was there again. He plunged for it, but not too eagerly. It was just as well that he had been cautious for the violet spurs were there again, ready for him. He sniffed haughtily. If they did not want him to leave their silly old path, that was all right by him!

The light that trickled through the filmy fern-trees was pale violet and the Colonel, paying as little attention as possible to his own feelings of strangeness, kept putting different filters on his camera. He took each photograph several times

40

and made a careful note after each exposure. He was trying to find out which filter would compensate for the light which was so different from that of Earth, or even of the Moon.

He seemed to be terribly excited by the strange appearance of the plants. Flyball could see nothing to get excited about. He, himself, was rather bewildered and annoyed than excited. The plants seemed to be shutting him in and when he looked back behind him he could no longer see the path down which they had come. It occurred to him that, if the plants wanted to do so, they could well prevent the two of them from finding their way back to the *Halley*. The plants were so tall that Colonel Stone would not be able to see over them. From his own experience Flyball knew that they could make a wall almost impossible to get through.

Then he cheered up. The plants did not know that Fred Stone was carrying a large and sharp knife on his hip. This would hack a way through the stoutest plants on Earth, and it should do the same on Venus.

Flyball gave a snooty snort at the plants nearest to him. It sounded terribly loud in the utter silence and the plants shuddered slightly. Ah, ha, Flyball thought, they know that we can get the better of them if we want to! He sauntered a little farther up the path after Fred Stone, waving his beautiful grey tail and purring softly to himself, just to show the plants that he did not care and that he had got their number.

The Colonel was intent upon taking a photograph of a large blue flower which looked as though it had been made from strips of rag. The flower was behaving in the strangest manner. It bobbed this way and that. Then it would pause and, just as Fred Stone had his camera focussed, it would bob its head again. Coy plants, thought Flyball, and decided against catching up with the Colonel.

He thought it would be pleasant to stretch himself after his long flight. He drove his long sharp claws into the ground. It felt a little like firm putty, which Flyball had seen the men using in fitting windows on the houses on the Moon. But, unlike putty, when he lifted his claws, he found that it had not stuck to his pads or fur. Also, the holes he made in the ground filled up as soon as he took his claws out of them.

He padded around a little clearing. There was no dust here either, he noted. It would be easy in this world for a cat to keep clean.

He sat down and gazed after the Colonel, who was still having difficulty with the shy flower. There was complete silence. Suddenly, Flyball seemed to hear a voice in his head. It was not at all the way he was accustomed to hear voices, for it had not spoken out loud as Fred Stone would have done, so Flyball knew it had nothing to do with him.

"Hello, stranger," the voice seemed to say, "are you the boss of this expedition?"

"Certainly, voice, most certainly!" Flyball thought back without the least hesitation.

Everyone knows that cats are *always* the bosses, no matter where they may find themselves. Then Flyball scratched behind his left ear as he considered that he was not being altogether fair.

"Well," he allowed thoughtfully, "there's also Fred Stone. That's him ahead of me, trying to take photographs. I brought him along with me to fly the machine and he thinks *he* is the boss. That's all the fault of these people back in Luna Port. They gave *him* command of the *Halley!*"

"Good," the thought came with perhaps the faintest hint of a chuckle. "Bring him back here."

Flyball scratched behind his right ear. There was something going on which he could not quite understand. He looked at the Colonel who, a few paces ahead, was busy taking shots of the bobbing flower with the shortest possible exposure. It was all very well for the "thought" to tell Flyball to bring back the Colonel, but that guy had a will of his own and might well refuse to come. However, there was no reason why he should not try.

"Miaow!" he said as loudly as he could. All the plants shuddered back violently, drawing away from him as if the sound disturbed or hurt them.

Flyball, who had always believed he had a most melodious miaow, felt rather put out by this behavior of the plants. He would have liked to ask who the plants thought they were? Music critics, perhaps? If so they were poor creatures, with no taste, who could not appreciate the delightful voice of a cat, and a spacecat at that!

"If that really is the only way you can get him," the thought seemed shaken, "you'd better try again."

"Mia-er-ow!" Flyball went, even more piercingly, while the plants shook and trembled even more violently than before.

Fred Stone looked back toward him. "What's up?" he called, and Flyball was comforted when he noticed that the Colonel's voice had just as disturbing an effect upon the plants as his own delightful one had had. Pods started bursting open all around him, with the softest of tinkles, throwing square purple seeds up into the air.

"Miaow!" went Flyball for the third time, rather more softly, so that the plants only shook a little. The Colonel walked slowly back along the path toward him.

Fred Stone, knowing that Flyball was a most intelligent cat, realized that he would not have called out unless it had been really necessary.

He came back to the clearing where the plants, driven back by the noise of Flyball's calling, had opened a space round him. The Colonel's camera was slung round his neck by a strap and he put it behind him in case Flyball needed help.

When Fred Stone reached Flyball he went down on one knee to see what could be the matter.

Then he looked up with a shocked expression on his face. He glanced wildly about him.

"Your boss here called you back," the thought had come into his mind. "We want to find out about you and your purpose here."

Colonel Stone looked at Flyball as if he suspected that his friend was playing

a very fancy kind of joke at his expense. But Flyball just sat there looking innocent, scratching at his ear, the left one again.

"Do you really mean that you cannot communicate sensibly with one another without all that horrible noise?" the thought went on. "Oh, you poor, poor creatures."

Following Flyball's example the bewildered Fred Stone tugged at the lobe of his ear. Then he shook his head as if to clear it.

"Who are you?" he thought hard. There did not seem to be any point in talking out loud, for the "thought" was certainly noiseless. Besides, he too had noticed that the plants did not like noises and, being a kind man, he did not want to make them any more uncomfortable than he could help.

"Look down," came the answering thought, and the Colonel looked down at Flyball who was polishing a whisker to show that, really, *he* was not in the least surprised.

Unfortunately for his show of disdain, he was polishing the same whisker over and over again as he thought that, since cats knew so much, it would be a pity to let even the Colonel suppose that they did not know all about everything.

"Flyball, you old fraud!" this time he knew it was the Colonel's thought and not the other. He jumped up in the air in surprise.

Colonel Stone was smiling as he examined a flat, dark green mossy plant with tiny white flowers. His knee had been resting on the edge of this. Now he put his finger against it.

"Yes," the thought was extremely strong. "I am the one who is in touch with you. When you put your knee on me and your friend, Flyball, had one

48

of his paws resting on me, *you were able to read his thoughts and send your own thoughts into his mind.* Should you wish to be able to go on doing this, just remove a fragment of my fringe and fasten it to your person and let your companion do the same. It will not hurt or damage me if you do this."

Obeying instructions, Fred Stone, with his knife, cut off two little pieces of the mossy plant. He slipped one of them under the strap of his wrist-watch and tied the other round Flyball's neck with a piece of tape he took from his pocket.

"Here's a fine how-do-you-do, Flyball" he thought. "Thought-reading plants! Are you getting my thoughts?"

"Of course I am," Flyball thought back in his most dignified manner. "I now know exactly what you're thinking. And I can't say I'm sure I like the idea of your being able to break in on all my private thoughts. How do you like the idea of me doing it to you?"

"Hmm. I can see what you mean. Things might get a little difficult," the Colonel allowed. "But, on the other hand, who would ever have supposed that we'd be able to stand here on Venus, exchang-

49

ing thoughts at all! And look at it from your own point of view, too, Flyball. Now you'll be able to let me know exactly what you need to make you comfortable. Up till now I've just had to guess. Now there'll be no more guesswork! Just think of that!"

"Yes, that's so, Fred," Flyball replied with great solemnity. "That is if you don't mind me calling you Fred, do you? After all you call me Flyball and I don't think of you as Colonel Frederick Stone!"

"Not at all, not at all!" Fred was polite, but his face still bore a bewildered expression as if he could not quite believe what was happening. He had been unable to adjust himself to the new situation as quickly as Flyball, who had taken it as if he had been swapping thoughts with humans all his life.

Once again Fred squatted down on the ground beside the dark moss with the tiny white star-like flowers. He remained there for hours, gathering information about Venus.

It seemed that, while on Earth the animals had become the intelligent form of life, exactly the opposite had happened on Venus. All around the planet the plants were able to communicate with one another, by exchanging thoughts, so that the plants in one place were able to find out almost at once what was happening in any other place. Even the seaweeds in the bright blue seas were able to play their part in this vast network of thought-exchanging.

As soon as the *Halley* had landed, the message that there were strangers on the planet had been passed around among the plants and now every plant on Venus was busy listening-in to the exchange between Fred and the little moss.

The only kind of animal that was to be found on the whole of Venus was a small blue mouse-like creature with a bushy tail and six legs.

Rather like a mouse, Flyball thought with satisfaction. Even if there were no birds on Venus, at least they *did* have something rather like a mouse!

"No," the thought seemed to shudder. "You mustn't chase them! They're harmless little creatures and we would not like to have them frightened. We use them for carrying pollen from one of us to the other, feeding them nectar in return, for they can travel more swiftly than we can, although, of course, we can move when we want to do so. Please do not worry them!"

51

Poor Flyball, who had forgotten for the moment that both the moss and Fred were listening-in on his thoughts, felt rather ashamed of himself and hastily promised that come what might, he would respect the rights of any and all Venusian mice whom he met, and that he would even go so far as to offer them the paw of friendship.

After all, he consoled himself, he was *the* Space Cat and could well afford to leave the chasing of mice to other, lesser, Earth-bound cats. Really, he told himself, mice were beneath his dignity. Birds, on the other hand, ah birds! Now *that* was another matter. Just wait till he caught up with some birds and he'd show them! A cat trained in space-flight could surely compete with a bird!

It was odd, he realized, that, while he and Fred could only read each other's thoughts as if they had been words, the moss seemed to be able to get pictures out of their minds, so that they did not have to explain to it what a bird was even though, until the arrival of the *Halley*, it had never seen a flying creature.

The only things that flew on Venus were the winged seeds of some of the plants. Although these seeds were not really intelligent like the fully-developed plants, they were able to soar and dip just like little gliders until they found a good place to land and put down their feeding-roots.

Fred was still making notes like mad when, suddenly and strongly, the moss forced a question into their minds, "Can you creatures live in ammonia?"

"Most certainly not!" the answering thought came vividly from them both.

"Well then you must hurry back to your ship. In a little time the ammonia rains will start. We need these rains, and you must remember to give these pieces of myself a daily drop of ammonia. Now you must hurry, for the rains are almost due!"

Fred jumped to his feet and set off through the jungle with Flyball perched on his shoulder. The plants opened a path before them, leading them back to the place on the shore where the *Halley* had landed. This was just as well, for with no sun to guide them they might have found it very hard to retrace their steps. The plants had closed the earlier path behind them and their feet had left no tracks on the rubbery ground.

Looking up, through a break in the fern-trees, Fred saw that the clouds were swirling lower and lower and he broke into a run, with Flyball on his

shoulder holding on for dear life. Flyball was aware that Fred was thinking that it would start to rain at any moment, and he himself was hoping in return that they would get back to the ship before they were caught in the threatening downpour. The plants seemed to sense their hurry and flung themselves aside as the Colonel ran toward them.

When at last they reached the beach they could see that the clouds now hung only a few hundred feet above the *Halley*. Fred scooted down the beach, kicking up the blue pebbles as he ran. Panting, he reached the side of the *Halley* and flung the door open. They had barely scrambled in, and had not yet had time to close the door when the first heavy drops of ammonia splashed on the ground and on the ship.

With a sigh of relief, Fred shut the door and they waited until the air-pressure in the air-lock was equal to that in the ship before once more entering the cabin.

"That was a narrow squeak," Fred thought, and Flyball agreed with him.

CHAPTER
FOUR

Once the rain really got going, there certainly was plenty of it. Even though they were snug inside the *Halley*, when they looked out through the uncovered glass ports, Flyball and Fred felt they could smell the pungent, throat-catching fumes of ammonia. Fred kept on jumping up to examine the dials that showed whether their air was pure. Naturally, none of the ammonia fumes could get into a ship which had been built to stand up to the emptiness of space. It was only the sight of the ammonia falling in sheets on the glass which made them feel as though they were smelling it.

After sitting around for sometime watching the downpour which made the worst cloudburst they had ever seen on Earth look like a summer shower, Fred turned to Flyball.

"I'm going to see if I can't make lockets for our moss," he announced without speaking. "If we go on carrying these little pieces around like this, one or other of us will be bound to lose his bit and then —bang goes our way of getting together!"

"Mmm. Yes," thought Flyball, "and it won't be a clever animal like a cat which will lose his piece, but a clumsy forgetful man!"

"Here, now," Fred returned. "That's not fair!"

"Sorry," Flyball was penitent. "I was thinking to myself. You're not supposed to have gotten that!"

Fred laughed. "I see what you meant when you thought there might be disadvantages to thinking out loud! Still, I suppose we'll always be able to take off the moss when we want to be private. That's still another reason for making lockets."

He went over to the side of the ship and opened a locker which was a beautifully fitted workshop, complete with lathes, drills, electric saws and everything else the builders of the *Halley* had thought they could possibly need to do repairs to the ship or make anything else they might want.

Drawers were filled with all kinds of materials—phosphor bronze, aluminum, stainless steel, brass, copper, plastics and the rest of them. Fred set to

58

work on a lathe and, before long, he had turned out two tiny bronze lockets with plastic faces, fastened to strong but slender chains. He fastened one of these round Flyball's neck and the other round his own.

Then, with the lockets dangling from their necks, they suddenly discovered that the exchange of thoughts was no longer taking place.

"That's odd," said Fred, taking his locket in his fingers and turning it.

The thought in his mind suddenly reached Flyball and he realized what the trouble had been. The Colonel, naturally, had hung the little lockets with the plastic faces out and the bronze next to their bodies. Flyball's locket, bouncing against him, had turned round, but Fred's had remained with the metal against his skin, until he touched the plastic with his fingers.

He then made adjustments to the chains which meant that they could keep their lockets either in the position for sending and receiving, or to obtain privacy.

As the drenching ammonia rain continued falling for hour after hour, they gradually got tired of the sight of it sloshing down the thick glass ports.

Finally Fred turned off the ship's lights and they relaxed in their hammocks.

Before Flyball fell asleep he carefully twiddled his locket round with his paws. *He* did not want to have the Colonel peeking in on his dreams, let alone his private falling-asleep thoughts.

When they awoke, the cabin was again bathed in the mysterious violet light and, looking out, they could see no signs of the ammonia rain which had poured down so heavily only a few hours before. It seemed, judging from the dials, that all the ammonia had been absorbed by the thirsty plants and ground.

After they had eaten their rations, they discussed the matter of further exploration.

Flyball was all in favor of returning home. "After all, Fred," he argued, "you've got enough to go on with. There'll be other expeditions and, besides, we're both due for leave. For leave on Earth —where there *are* birds!"

Fred sighed. "When *will* you forget these birds, Flyball? You know you'll never catch one. You're far too impatient. Besides, I don't suppose you'd know what to do with it if you *did* manage to lay your paws on one. Would you, now? It's just the challenge, isn't it?"

"Maybe," Flyball acknowledged the question gravely. "After all, it really *is* beneath my dignity to go off chasing poor Earth-bound creatures now I'm a seasoned spacecat. Still," he twitched an appreciative whisker, "I've got to teach those birds to stop being so cheeky!"

"All right," Fred came back, "you can do your bird-chasing when we get our leave. In the meantime, whatever you may have told our friends, I'm still officially boss of this expedition! Let me go my own way about finding out all I can about this strange planet Venus! Of course, it'll take a full-sized expedition to really do the job of exploring. Still, we may be able to find out things that'll make their job easier. Besides, first-comers get the first serving. And I'm interested. Anyhow, we have discovered that men must not interfere with the plants or the little animals. If we hadn't been lucky enough to find the moss so soon we might have made a lot of enemies. Let's get going!"

"*We* found the moss," Flyball thought, "you mean *I found.* . . ." Then, embarrassed, he realized that Fred was aware what he was thinking, and quickly sent on an apology.

Fred did not reply, but stood up and went toward the air-lock.

61

"Hey," Flyball was urgent, "aren't you forgetting something?"

Fred turned his head. "No." He was puzzled. "I don't think so."

"What about our little bits of moss and their daily dose of ammonia?" Flyball wanted to know, touching his locket with a gentle paw.

The Colonel nodded his head and opened the door of the lock.

Outside he examined the ground carefully for ammonia, but found that it had all sunk away through the blue pebbles. He walked to the edge of the sea and smelled the water cautiously. It had a faint smell of ammonia, but he did not think it would be strong enough for the moss. Finally, however, in a crevice on the *Halley*, he found a tiny pool which had been left from the torrential downpour.

He took a little bottle from his pocket and filled it with ammonia.

"You see," he explained to Flyball, who sat there looking wise, "we can't be sure that the ammonia here on Venus is exactly the same as that I've got in the chemical box on board the ship. I certainly wouldn't like to feed our little friends here," he fingered the locket, "anything that they wouldn't like."

He opened both their lockets and put a drop of ammonia on each of the fragments of moss. The smell was terribly strong and Flyball wrinkled his nose and twitched his whiskers as the fumes went up his nostrils. Then he sneezed.

"Really," he thought, once again forgetting that Fred was listening-in, "it would be much better if the moss only needed something nice, such as milk!"

"You *are* an ungrateful cat," he was told.

Flyball, offended, stuck his tail up in the air and slowly, with enormous dignity, went up the beach ahead of the Colonel. He wasn't going to stand still and let anyone insult him. Then he became aware that he had still forgotten to turn his locket round. Fred was laughing at him.

He switched his tail once or twice and then came to the conclusion that he might just as well give up his appearance of injured dignity. After all, there were only the two of them, some "mice" creatures and a lot of plants on the whole of the planet Venus. There was little doubt, that some-time he would get a chance to laugh at Colonel

Fred Stone and then, by golly, he really would laugh!

At the edge of the fern-tree forest, the "milk-weed" plants with the beautiful pods and the others again made way for them. This time, however, the thought seemed to have gone around that the visitors were really friendly, and that they were to be allowed to wander wherever they wanted to go. There was no attempt by the plants, as there had been earlier, to lead them in any special direction.

It seemed to Flyball, padding softly along beside Fred, that they went an awfully long way. Still, it did not feel so far, as the Colonel stopped whenever he wanted to take a photograph of a new and strange plant—and there were plenty of these. One of them was like a large red ball with tiny little green leaves, like rabbit-ears, sticking out at different places all over the bright globe, and another was a tall green stick with seven odd-shaped leaves, rather like a human hand with two extra fingers.

Fred, as he took his photographs, was aware that the plants were doing their best to help him. All the way they received whispered thoughts from the plants, passing the word from one to the other, "All's well. They are friends."

They knew, from what the moss had told them, that this word had been passed all round the planet and the feeling of silent peacefulness all round them was wonderful. No matter where they went on Venus they would find that the plants were friendly.

Fred was busy taking a color-photograph of a plant that looked rather like a vast tangled skein of different colored wools, with odd magenta knobs scattered through it. Flyball was amusing himself by trying to make his whiskers twitch in time with the bursting of a yellow plant's brown pods. Suddenly he became aware that the plants round him were disturbed. He was not as preoccupied as Fred, so that the thoughts came to him clearly.

"Oh, no, no," the plants were thinking. "Keep it away! Keep it away!"

If there was one thing of which Flyball had more than his fair share it was curiosity. He peeked through the stems of the plants which had huddled together. In the middle of a clearing made by the withdrawal of the friendly plants he saw the most appalling thing.

It was a kind of walking plant, standing on about fifty legs, each of them shaped somewhat like a banana. From the black center, where these legs joined, there arose thick red leaf-stems which finished in round flat pads, green tinged with pink. On each of the pads there were dozens of feelers, ending in round sucker-tips.

One of these pads held a little animal, pale blue in color, with six legs and a bushy, darker blue, tail. The little animal's eyes were round with terror.

The plant was swaying backwards and forwards, just holding the little creature there as if pleased with its capture.

Flyball remembered what the moss had told him the day before. These little "mice" were the friends of the plants and yet *this* plant was frightening one of them. Then, too, all the other plants seemed to be frightened and shocked. This meant that the horrible-looking plant was an enemy.

Besides, Flyball went on to himself, if *he* was obeying orders in not hunting the little blue animals, the wicked plant had no right to catch one. He, Flyball, was a cat and as such had the first rights to all mice and other small game. If he could behave himself in the presence of mice he did not see why others should be allowed to misbehave.

"Miaow! Scraww!" he howled and hurled himself toward the plant, unsheathing his claws as he did so.

Unlike the other Venusian plants, this one did not shudder at the fearful noise. It flipped a lazy pad toward him. Flyball ripped at it. The pad jerked back and he took a good hard swipe at the thick red stem of the pad which held the blue mouse.

He managed to cut it almost half-way through with his sharp claws and slowly, ever so slowly, it drooped toward the ground. It did not, however, let go of the little animal.

Flyball was just about to take another slash at the stem, to finish cutting it in halves, when one of the pads grabbed him by the side. He had to turn his claws and his teeth on this attacker. Even as he clawed and tore, doing terrific damage to the pad which held him, another pad clutched him. It seemed that the plant was willing to let the little blue creature rest provided it could capture this much bigger and fatter victim.

He was ripping away with his razor-sharp claws, tearing at the red-stems, but he could not get into the black core of the plant. More and more pads were gripping him on every part of the body. They hindered him in his work of destruction. Now he became aware that the plant was moving over the ground on its banana-like legs, dragging both him and the blue mouse along with it. A lucky slash caught the center, the black core, and for a moment, as the plant shuddered, Flyball thought he had won.

But, from the black heart there sprouted more

tentacles which fastened on to him, so that he was nearly helpless. At the same time, he realized that the plant, never having had to deal with a real fighter such as he was, was gradually weakening.

He redoubled his efforts, at the same time sending calls of help to Fred. Then he felt the rubbery ground shaking as Fred ran toward him.

Peeking out from under a pad which covered one of his eyes, he saw that Fred had drawn his gun. The pads, however, were waving about so violently that it would have been impossible to risk a shot without fear of hitting either Flyball or the little creature.

"Use your knife, Fred," Flyball thought urgently. "Hit it in the black core."

Fred slipped his gun back into his holster and, drawing his knife, approached cautiously. He slashed at the pads which held Flyball and they drooped to the ground, as the plant turned its attention to this new attacker. Whatever the plant was it was certainly brave. It tried to cling to Fred and succeeded in hampering him so that he could not get the knife into the core. But in doing so the plant neglected Flyball.

Suddenly he sprang, spitting and clawing, right

into the center. He tore at it ferociously. The banana-legs sprawled sideways and the pads fell limply to the ground. The plant was dead.

Free, the little blue animal stood upon four of its six legs with the other two held in front of it, looking at Flyball who had, so unexpectedly, rescued it.

"Hmm," thought Flyball, smoothing down his fur where it had been ruffled by the pads. "Who'd have thought of me as the rescuer of *mice*. I just hope this doesn't get around among my friends on Earth!" He looked at the little creature. "You'd better buzz, pal, while I remember that I'm on my best behavior, and before I begin to think that you're only a mouse—even if you *do have* six legs and are bright blue. I can't go on being too respectable for too long!"

"Hey, Flyball," it was Fred, "remember your manners! These mice are O-U-T—OUT!"

The little blue creature put an end to possible argument by winking its dark ruby-red eyes as if in gratitude and then disappearing suddenly among the plants, which once again were drawing near to Flyball and Fred.

The dead plant, on the ground, was quickly

turning into a slimy jelly which was absorbed by the putty-like surface of the planet. They turned to the other plants.

Before them was a patch of the dark green moss with the tiny white flowers. They drew near to it and Fred stooped down toward it, with Flyball sitting beside him.

"I'm really sorry if we've done something we shouldn't have done," Fred thought. "But it seemed to be a case of that plant or Flyball."

"That's all right," the moss replied. "In fact, we're all grateful to you and are delighted that we have found friends who can deal with our only enemy. The *ygrombumia* is an enemy plant. We are peaceful but it is warlike. It destroys as many of us and as many of the *snoryus*—the little blue animals—as it can. We, the plants, have learned to avoid it, or

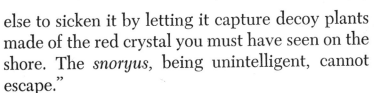

else to sicken it by letting it capture decoy plants made of the red crystal you must have seen on the shore. The *snoryus*, being unintelligent, cannot escape."

"Wait a moment," Fred was excited. "You mean to say that you can actually *work* the red crystals? Why—they broke the point of my diamond!"

73

"Why, of course we can," the moss was matter of fact. "It melts easily in the juice of the *tlora*—the filmy fern-trees. But, to go on, there are very few of the *ygrombumia* left. I don't suppose there are more than half-a-dozen on the whole planet. You, with your weapons, could wipe them out easily enough."

"Yes," Fred agreed, "but next time I think I'll stay out of reach and use a gun. What do you think, Flyball?"

Flyball, who was still feeling a little peeved by the picture of himself as a brave rescuer of mice, agreed.

The moss, seeming to cut its thoughts off from them, paused. Then it went on, "Word of your success has gone out all over Venus and all the plants wish to express their gratitude to their new friends who can defeat our only enemy. We don't really know what we can do to show our thankfulness—unless it is to give you a banquet."

The Colonel looked surprised. "Um, yes," he was slow. "That's a very kind offer, but what *could* we eat? After all, we don't want to eat any of you plants, and the only other life is the *snoryus*. And we certainly don't want to eat them either, eh, Flyball?"

Flyball, who was on his best behavior, agreed with him and went on washing his face. By thinking hard of the problems of smoothing his fine fur, he was able to keep from thinking that he, for one, would not object to a tasty dish of *snoryus.*

"Oh," the moss was sympathetic, but it seemed to think they had less intelligence than it had previously given them credit for, "we can give you nectar to drink and, then, just so long as you don't eat the seeds and see that they're planted properly, there's plenty of fruit around, as well as other things."

CHAPTER
FIVE

It was certainly the strangest feast that either Flyball or Fred had ever attended, and they had been to plenty after their first flight to the Moon.

They sat upon the springy ground surrounded by all kinds of plants and ate the food which was brought to them by relays of plants, which passed it rapidly from one to the other, right from the other side of Venus, through the forests and jungles, over the seas and lakes.

The food was wonderful. The moss had examined their minds to find the foods they liked best. Flyball, for instance was given a large cream-colored fruit, which, much to his surprise, had the texture of and tasted exactly like boiled cod. Fred was given a thick leaf which, when the green rind was peeled off, left him holding a slice of something which was, so far as he could tell, exactly the same as rare roast beef.

For drink they were served a slightly sweetish liquid in the cup-shaped leaves of a kind of water-lily.

Even though Flyball had never imagined himself enjoying a vegetarian meal, he had to admit that the meal they were eating was indeed excellent.

While they ate they talked, in thought, with their hosts. This kind of conversation had the great advantage that it could be carried on with one's mouth full, without any appearance of rudeness.

It seemed that the *ygrombumia* plants were not native to Venus, at least so far as the history remembered by the other plants went. The moss had a theory that, several hundred years earlier, the seeds of the *ygrombumia* had somehow wandered through space, and had drifted in through the clouds and found the climate of Venus suited them.

"Hmm," thought Flyball, the Space Cat, "space seeds!" But he went on paying attention.

The plants had always been willing to suppose that, even if they could not imagine it, there had to be some other place beyond the clouds. One of the reasons they had been worried by the arrival of the *Halley*, with Flyball and Fred on board, had been that they feared it might mean that their world was being invaded by *plants* even more ferocious than the *ygrombumia*. In that case, they would have had to think of new methods of dealing with such enemies.

Of course, never, even in their wildest dreams, had the plants been able to think it possible that *animals*, such as the *snoryus*, could be the guiding brains behind such a ship. They still found it difficult to understand that, on Earth, the smallest animal was more intelligent than the largest tree.

"Perhaps," the moss, whose name was *pyxyx*, asked, "the trouble is that you have failed to get in touch with your plants and are therefore unable to understand their minds?"

"Perhaps," Fred allowed doubtfully, "but in that case I'm afraid we must have caused a great deal of trouble in the vegetable kingdom. Men have, over the last few thousand years, taken wild plants, such as the potato, maize, oats, carrots and the rest of them, and have bred them into plants for their own use. Still, I must say that I don't think that the earthly domesticated cabbage could possibly be sensible. What do you think, Flyball?"

Flyball, who had no affection for cabbage, or at least no more than most cats, agreed that vegetables on Earth were completely lacking in sense. Furthermore, he wished it understood that a good many Earth animals, notably dogs, were also short of real brains.

Fred laughed as he explained to the plants the odd fact that dogs and cats did not, as a general rule, get along well together on Earth. The sound of Fred's laughter seemed to upset the plants almost as much as the noise they had made earlier had done.

Then, too, the plants could not understand why a man should be amused by the thought of two intelligent creatures quarrelling. Fred tried to explain that his laughter had been caused, not by the thought of strife, but by Flyball's prim self-righteousness. The more Fred tried to explain about Earth and its attitude to wars, the more puzzled the plants became.

Finally *pyxyx*, who seemed to be looked upon

by the other plants as a wise counsellor, made a suggestion.

"Why don't you collect the seeds out of the fruit you have eaten and take them back to Earth with you? They will grow easily if you remember they have to be given ammonia daily. Then, when they are fully grown, and have had a chance to observe the world around them, you can bring them back here and they will report to us?"

"That seems a good idea," if Fred was amused by the thought of plants observing and reporting on men, he was careful not to show it, "but once the plants grow I don't think the botanists will like having to give up their charges. Perhaps you'd better give us several seeds of each kind so that there will be enough to go round."

The plants nodded in silence for a few moments and neither Flyball nor Fred could catch their thoughts. Finally, however, they found they were being presented with seeds which had been brought at express speed from wherever the plants grew. Fred put each lot of seeds in a separate envelope and on the outside he wrote the name which *pyxyx* told him.

All this took a long time and then *pyxyx* made a

request. "But there is one thing further we must ask of you. You must not divide your portions of me with others. We would like to keep to ourselves the right to give thought-exchange to those whom we think deserve it. You, as our friends and the slayers of the *ygrombumia,* can keep your own pieces, but we would like you not to talk about them. Is that all right?"

Flyball and Fred thought this was a reasonable request, but the latter wondered how he could explain the plants and their ways on Venus to his superiors. *Pyxyx* broke in on his thoughts.

"You can, of course, explain that we were able to exchange thoughts with you. You must, in fact, do this, for if others of your kind come here we wish to be able to live in peace with them. And," the thought was a little wistful, "it may be that those others, able to move all about the planet, will, with our help, hunt down the last of the *ygrombumia?*"

"Of course they will," Fred responded. "We would do it ourselves, but our ship does not move easily from place to place for short distances. Now," he glanced at his watch, "I'm afraid that we'll have to go back to the ship to avoid the rains."

83

They said good-bye to their new-found friends. It was a sad parting for they had become fond of the plants. Then they returned to the *Halley*, without having to hurry. Fred placed a large jar with a funnel in it, on the ground outside to collect enough ammonia to give their *pyxyx* its daily ration for years, even if they had not returned to Venus before then.

When the rains stopped they went out of the ship only as far as the *tlora* trees and, after asking politely, they were given a large quantity of juice, which poured in a yellow stream from little holes in the bark.

It was as *pyxyx* had told them. The juice, which did not hurt paws or hands when dipped in it, cut through the harder-than-diamond crystal like a stream of hot water on butter. They collected a large quantity of the red chunks for Fred was certain that men, back on Earth, would find them of the greatest value, and they also filled a box with the bright blue pebbles, which did not melt in *tlora* juice.

They placed the large glass jar of ammonia and a small jar of *tlora* juice in a foam-rubber lined closet, where they packed them tight with more foam-rubber, to make sure they were not knocked about and broken.

Then they prepared for the take-off. They got into their suits and put on their goldfish-bowl helmets. They were delighted to find that the *pyxyx* still allowed them to exchange thoughts through the heavy plastic.

Flyball, it must be admitted, grumbled like anything at having to put on his space-suit, even though he knew that it was necessary. This was the first time, however, that his friend had had his opinions on the matter.

"It's all right, I agree with you," Fred was sympathetic, "but if we're to go bounding around in space we've got to wear them till we know that everything's going right. I don't like my suit any more than you do, but, if anything goes wrong, they'll give us a chance. Come on, Space Cat!"

Flyball was ashamed of himself for grumbling, and let Fred tighten the wing-nuts that held his helmet in place.

Once dressed and with everything checked, they fixed themselves in their hammocks. Fred pressed the buttons and the pulsing roar of the rockets grew louder and louder and the *Halley*

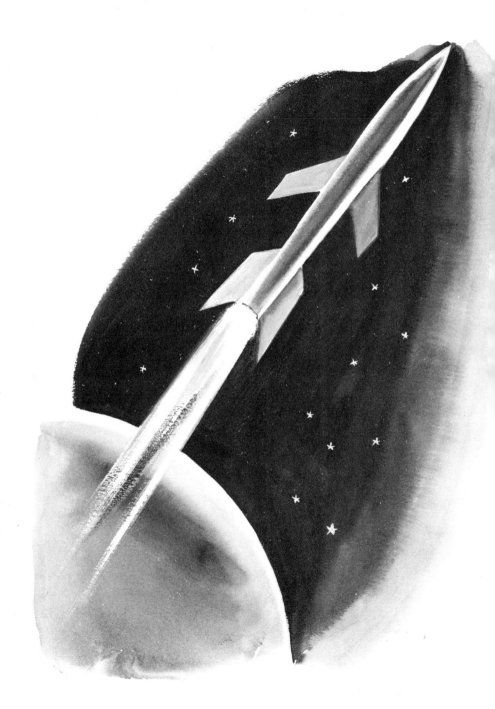

shuddered violently. Then, with a sudden whoosh, they rose from the surface of Venus, climbing steeply in the air toward the clouds, getting faster all the time.

Flyball, who had nothing to do, snoozed quietly, dreaming of the wonderful things that could happen to a spacecat.

Z